UNR

CuteTitos

A FURRY FRIEND

™

THE ULTIMATE CHARACTER GUIDE-ito

by Marilyn Easton

PENGUIN YOUNG READERS LICENSES
An Imprint of Penguin Random House LLC, New York

Cutetitos is a trademark of Basic Fun, Inc. © 2020 Basic Fun, Inc.
Boca Raton, Florida 33431, USA

Published by Penguin Young Readers Licenses,
an imprint of Penguin Random House LLC, New York. Manufactured in China.

Visit us online at www.penguinrandomhouse.com.

ISBN 9780593095652   10 9 8 7 6 5 4 3 2 1

This bookito
belongs to

_____

CONTENTITOS

WELCOME TO THE WORLDITO OF CUTETITOS™

Cutetitos are cuddly frienditos who love taking burrito naps. But they won't stay asleep for long! Once you unwrap them, they're ready to meet you and are up for any adventure! When your Cutetito wants to take their next burrito nap, just wrap them up snugly in their burrito blanket. They'll look so warm and comfy, you might even want to wrap yourself up, too!

There's a whole world of Cutetitos out there for you to meet. There are feathered frienditos, like Flamingitos and Parrotitos. Some Cutetitos, like the Sealitos and Dolphinitos, come from the sparkling ocean. The wildest Cutetitos, like Zebritos and Cheetaritos, can't get enough playtime, while Catitos and Puppitos prefer taking extra-long naps and having lots of snuggle time. There are even Babitos, baby Cutetitos, who love being cuddled and hugged!

Get to know all the Cutetitos and Babitos—their names, birthdays, types of animalito, Hot Spot Spice-O-Meter levels, unique personalities, and more-ito!

Collecting CUTETITOS™

There are so many different Cutetitos to unwrap and collect, it can be hard to keep track of them all!

There are different ways to collect Cutetitos: You can start with collecting one type of Cutetito, like all the Puppitos. Or you can try to collect all the Cutetitos who are Medium on the Hot Spot Spice-O-Meter. Or you can just collect them all! There's really no wrong way to collect Cutetitos, as long as you're having fun!

Trading Tip

If you unwrap a Cutetito that you already have, ask your frienditos if they'd like to trade! You can use this book to keep track of all your Cutetitos, so you don't accidentally trade for one that's already in your collection!

Hot Spot Spice-O-Meter

Each Cutetito comes with a Hot Spot. The Hot Spot looks like a sparkly chili pepper and tells you how rare that type of Cutetito is! Orange Hot Spots are the most common, while pink Hot Spots are very rare. All Cutetitos have a spicy kick to them, although some have more than others! Use the following guide to learn more about your Cutetito's Hot Spot.

HOT SPOT SPICE-O-METER MILD

Examples of Mild Cutetitos

Huggito   Bellito   Tabbito

These are the most common Cutetitos, but just because they're mild doesn't mean they're ordinary! Cutetitos with a Mild Hot Spot can't wait to be woken up from their siesta slumber so they can meet you!

Examples of Medium Cutetitos

Oinkito　　Shellito　　Houndito

Cutetitos with a Medium Hot Spot are the second most common type of Cutetito. If you unwrap one of these Cutetitos, be prepared to have a ton of funito and get a lot of huggitos!

Examples of Hot Cutetitos

Frostito　　Zippito　　Wildito

Unwrapping a Hot Hot Spot Cutetito is pretty rare, but with enough luck, you're sure to unroll one eventually! And once you do, you've got a friendito for life.

Examples of Super Spicy Cutetitos

Cheekito　　Hefftito　　Cloudito

Cutetitos with a Super Spicy Hot Spot are ultra-rare! These extra-special Cutetitos can be hard to find, so once you unwrap one, hold on to it tightly!

CuteTitos™
Name Generator

Have you ever wondered what your unique Cutetitos

name would be? Follow the directions to find out!

Name:

_____

_____

_____

_____

_____

DIRECTIONS

FIRST NAME: Add "-ito" to the end of your first name.

MIDDLE NAME: Add "-ito" to the end of your favorite color.

LAST NAME: Find the first letter of your last name
to see your Cutetitos last name.

Now try it with the names of your family and frienditos!

A - Crazito   J - Hotito   S - Goofito

B - Hangrito   K - Grumpito   T - Sweetito

C - Slopito   L - Sillyito   U - Smartito

D - Freshito   M - Hyperito   V - Chillito

E - Lazito   N - Boldito   W - Clownito

F - Funito   O - Friendlito   X - Sleepito

G - Stinkito   P - Hungrito   Y - Messito

H - Sassito   Q - Gigglito   Z - Crankito

I - Wackito   R - Happito

PEPPER PLEDGE

Wrap yourself in your blanket
(like a burrito!) and state the following:

"I, _____,
promise to take care of my Cutetitos.
Whether they're spicy, hot, medium, or mild,
I vow to love them, no matter how wild.
I'll chill with them and wrap them tight.
Soooo cute, I'll want to take a bite . . .
but I won't."

Give your Cutetito a hug to seal the promise.

_____
Date

_____
Signature

_____
Your Cutetitos Name

How to Unwrap a Cutetito

Unwrapping your Cutetito is a magical moment, since it's the first time you're meeting each other! No matter which method you choose, there's really no wrong way to unwrap a Cutetito! Here are some ideas on how to unroll your new friendito.

The Traditionalito

As soon as you get your Cutetito, unwrap it immediately! After all, how can you stand to wait any longer to meet your new bestito?

The Dance-ito

Think of your absolute favorite song of all time. Now pump up the tunes. Not loud enough? Turn up the volume-ito! Grab your Cutetito, and start unwrapping as you dance.

The Upside-Downito

On a sofa or chair, put your back where you normally sit, lift your legs and point them in the air, and let your head hang off the seat. You should now be upside-downito. Now, unwrap your Cutetito, and let the topsy-turvy fun begin!

The Super Surprise-ito

Do you want an extra surprise while unwrapping your Cutetito? While standing, hold your Cutetito behind your back. Start unwrapping. How long can you wait before you see which Cutetito you unwrapped?

Extra Challenge-ito

Have a friendito stand behind you as you unwrap your Cutetito. Then, start guessing which one it is! Once your friendito confirms you've guessed correctly, meet your Cutetito!

○ Bellito™   ● Cheekito™   ○ Despacito™

○ Fluffito™   ○ Frostito™   ○ Hoppito™

Super Rare

MILD MEDIUM HOT SUPER SPICY

○ Luckito™

○ Oinkito™

○ Pawsito™

○ Peppito™

○ Speedito™

○ Sweetito™

Name:
Bellito™

Birthday: November 18

MILD

Type of Animalito:
Puppito™

Favorite Quotito:
"Happiness is a HUGGITO!"

Secret Factito

Bellito can sometimes be a little shy, but once she gets to know you, you'll be best palitos! She loves playing outside, eating tasty treats, and getting loving huggitos. Her favorite way to wake up from a burrito nap is with a big stretch and a huggito from a friend. When you meet her for the first time, just try to be quiet and calm, otherwise you might scare her a little.

Name:
Cheekito™

Birthday: December 14

Super Rare

SUPER SPICY

Favorite Quotito:
"I like to GUAC 'N' ROLL!"

Type of Animalito:
Monkito™

Secret Factito

Cheekito can play five different instruments . . . at the same time! He's always up for a jam session with frienditos and enjoys combining different styles of music. This Monkito even writes some of his own songs! His favorites to perform are "I'm Bananas for Bananas" and "My Nana Is a Banana"!

Despacito

Birthday: October 20

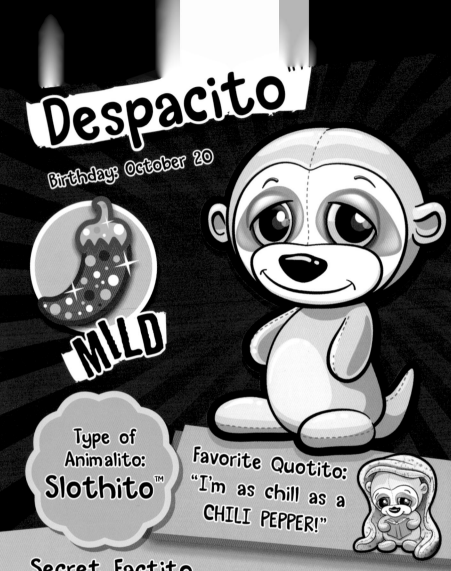

MILD

Type of Animalito:
Slothito™

Favorite Quotito:
"I'm as chill as a CHILI PEPPER!"

Secret Factito

Despacito is an expertito at chilling out and living life in the slow lane. He's a low-key Slothito who takes every day (every minute, really) as it comes. His favorite activity is napping and lying around with his eyes closed (which is really just more napping). Even if he gets woken up from his nappito, he won't get upset—he just closes his eyes and keeps on dreaming.

Name: Fluffito™

Birthday: June 21

HOT

Favorite Quotito:
"Let's TACO about it!"

Type of Animalito:
Puppito™

Secret Factito

Fluffito will always lend a helping paw to her frienditos. Whether you need a study buddy for a big testito or a cheerleader to get you past the finish line, you can count on this Puppito! She's also a really good listener and loves to give helpful advice to her frienditos whenever they may need it.

Name:
Frostito™

Birthday: September 9

HOT

Type of
Animalito:
Bearito™

Favorite Quotito:
"Free HUGGITOS!"

Secret Factito

Frostito gives the best Bearito huggitos! A huggito from Frostito can make even a snowman feel warm and cuddly inside. This Bearito believes in spreading the love, even if sometimes her arms get tired from too much hugging. She set the Cutetitos recordito for most huggitos given in a single day—fifty-two!

Name: Hoppito™

Birthday: April 21

MEDIUM

Favorite Quotito:
"This is how I ROLLITO!"

Type of Animalito:
Bunnito™

Secret Factito

Hoppito has caught the travel bugito. He loves hopping around different cities and is always the first to jump into any adventure. He always has his camera packed in his bagito so he can take pictures to show his frienditos.

Name:
Luckito™

Birthday: August 17

HOT

Type of
Animalito:
Catito™

Favorite Quotito:
"You GUAC my world!"

Secret Factito

Luckito is a super-lucky Cutetito. If you scratch Luckito behind her ear, she'll bring you good luck. And if you give her a belly rubito, she might even give you extra good luck! Basically, any time you pet Luckito, it's your lucky day!

Name: Oinkito™

Birthday: March 1

MEDIUM

Favorite Quotito:
"Neato BURRITO!"

Type of
Animalito:
Pigito™

Secret Factito

Ever since she was little, Oinkito has been amazed at the world. She's been studying all the incredible things that can happen in nature. She tries to make a new discovery every day—there's just so many wonders to uncover! When she finds something new, she cheers, "Neato BURRITO!"

Name:
Pawsito™

Birthday: February 17

MILD

Type of
Animalito:
Catito™

Favorite Quotito:
"I'm NACHO average
Cutetito!"

Secret Factito

Pawsito is loud and proud, but that's just because he knows
he's the cat's meowito! He's all about self-love, self-care,
and paw fives, and has major love in his heart for his family
and frienditos. His ultimate goal: make all the Cutetitos feel

Name:
Peppito™

Birthday: May 14

MEDIUM

Favorite Quotito:
"Life is BURRITOFUL!"

Type of Animalito:
Chihuahito™

Secret Factito

Peppito always looks on the bright side, no matter what.
Even on a rainy day, he finds a way to have funito. You can
find him jumping in puddles and making a big splashito!
This Chihuahito always has pep in his step and can turn any
bad day into an awesome one!

Name:
Speedito™

Birthday: July 11

HOT

Type of
Animalito:
Slothito™

Favorite Quotito:
"Let's have a
slumber PARTITO!"

Secret Factito

If there's a Cutetitos party, Speedito will be the first to arrive
and the last to leave. He loves costume partitos, birthday
partitos, pool partitos—really any partito is his favorite!
Slothitos may have a reputation for living life a little more
slowly than other Cutetitos, but not Speedito! If you attend
one of his slumber partitos, prepare to pull an all-nighter.

Name:
Sweetito™

Birthday: January 2

Super Rare
↳

SUPER SPICY

Favorite Quotito:
"It's FIESTA time!"

Type of Animalito:
Catito™

Secret Factito

Sweetito can turn any situation into a full-on fiesta. Is it three o'clock on a Wednesday afternoon? Then it's time for a fiesta. Did you just blink your eyes three times in a row? Then it's time for a fiesta. Fiesta time is all the time for this party animalito. Even when she takes her burrito naps, she's dreaming about one thing—fiestas!

 ◯ Floppito™

 ● Fuzzito™

 ● Gracito™

 ● Hefftito™

 ◯ Huggito™

 ◯ Jazzito™

MILD

MEDIUM

HOT

Super Rare

SUPER SPICY

○ Jokito™

● Shellito™

○ Sparklelito™

○ Surfito™

○ Woofito™

● Zippito™

Name:
Floppito™

Birthday: May 8

HOT

Type of
Animalito:
Donkito™

Favorite Quotito:
"SPICE to meet you!"

Secret Factito

Floppito loves all things spicito. No matter the food, she always adds extra-spicy hot sauce with chili flakes sprinkled on top. This Donkito has been the champion of the Cutetitos hot-pepper eating contest for three years in a row!

34

Name: Fuzzito™

Birthday: November 17

MEDIUM

Favorite Quotito:
"Bon Appétito!"

Type of Animalito:
Bearito™

Secret Factito

Fuzzito is an excellent chef and loves cooking his frienditos their favorite meals. He's won several Top Chefito awards and hopes to write a cookbook one day featuring all his favorite recipes and cooking tipitos. His best recipe ideas come to him while he is taking his burrito nap, so if he is sleeping, try not to wake him!

Name:
Gracito™

Birthday: February 23

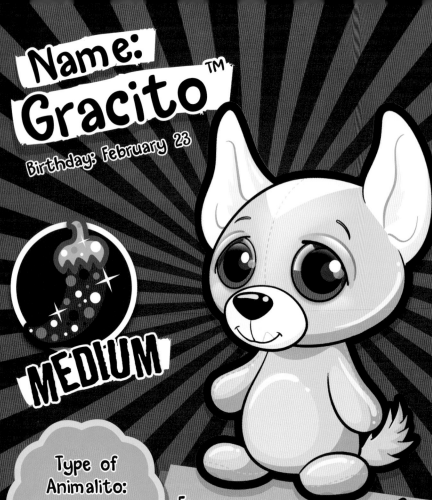

MEDIUM

Type of
Animalito:
Chihuahito™

Favorite Quotito:
"I'm the life of
the PARTITO!"

Secret Factito

Gracito is always the first to step onto the dance floor! This
Chihuahito has her ultimate dance playlist ready to go at
all times and knows how to keep the partito going. She can
party-hop and dance the night away better than anyone!

Name:
Hefftito™

Birthday: August 12

Super Rare

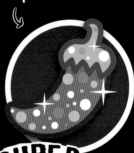

SUPER SPICY

Favorite Quotito:
"I've GUAC
you covered!"

Type of
Animalito:
Elephantito™

Secret Factito

Hefftito dreams BIG. She believes she can accomplish anything if she sets her mindito to it! If a friendito shares their dreams with her, she'll encourage them to dream even bigger and help them achieve their goalitos.

Name:
Huggito™

Birthday: January 26

MILD

Type of Animalito:
Koalito™

Favorite Quotito:
"LETTUCE be frienditos!"

Secret Factito

Huggito believes you can never have too many frienditos. He loves meeting new people and learning all about them. It helps that he never forgets a name! This Koalito has helped many Cutetitos make new frienditos and form clubs based on their interests. He loves seeing all his frienditos getting along!

Name:
Jazzito™

Birthday: October 29

MILD

Favorite Quotito:
"Let's SALSA the night away!"

Type of Animalito:
Catito™

Secret Factito

Jazzito is a talented, classically trained dancer who loves being center stage and in the spotlight. He can perform any type of dance, from elegant ballet to spicy salsa, but his favorite type of dance is jazz. He choreographs his own dance routines and hopes to one day perform on his very own world tourito!

Name: Jokito™

Birthday: March 19

HOT

Type of Animalito:
Parrotito™

Favorite Quotito:
"GUAC GUAC!
Who's there?"

Secret Factito

Jokito loves telling jokes and making her frienditos laugh!
This Parrotito is working on her stand-up comedy routine and
writing new jokes every day. Her favorite soundito is laughter,
and her favorite type of jokes to tell are Guac Guac jokes.

Name:
Shellito™

Birthday: December 27

MEDIUM

Favorite Quotito:
"Listen to your HEARTITO!"

Type of Animalito:
Turtleito™

Secret Factito

Shellito can sometimes come off as sensitive, but every day he tries to come out of his shell a little more-ito. Some of his frienditos think he wears his heart on his shell, but this Turtleito can't help sharing his feelings. His favorite kind of movies are romantic comedies—he's always rooting for a happy ending.

41

Name:
Sparklelito™

Birthday: June 4

Super Rare

SUPER
SPICY

Type of
Animalito:
Catito™

Favorite Quotito:
"If you've got it,
FLAUNTITO it!"

Secret Factito

Sparklelito may be all glitz and glam, but when she isn't walking the red carpetito, she is really down-to-earth and likes watching movies with her frienditos. If this Catito has an event to attend, it takes her an entire day to get ready, with hair, makeup, and wardrobe. But Sparklelito doesn't mind—she loves getting all dressed up!

Name:
Surfito™

Birthday: June 2

Super Rare
↳

SUPER SPICY

Favorite Quotito:
"Let's make a SPLASHITO!"

Type of Animalito:
Dolphinito™

Secret Factito

Surfito is really playful, especially when it comes to water activities. She loves relay races in the water with her frienditos and always takes a challenge to see how many flippitos she can do before she gets dizzy (so far her record is fifteen). She may not be the fastest ocean-dwelling Cutetito, but she knows how to have the most funito!

Woofito ™

Birthday: July 1

MILD

Type of Animalito:
Puppito ™

Favorite Quotito:
"Did someone say BURRITO DAY?"

Secret Factito

Every day is a celebration for Woofito! He believes in celebrating all things big and small. His favorite celebration is the first Thursday in April, which is National Burrito Day! Every year he hosts a big party with games like pin the tomato on the burrito, and a burrito sack race!

Name:
Zippito™

Birthday: April 10

HOT

Favorite Quotito:
"Let the good times ROLLITO!"

Type of Animalito:
Narwhalito™

Secret Factito

Zippito loves living in the sparkling oceanito. Every morning when he wakes up, he goes for a swim around the beautiful coral reef near his home. Zippito swims so fast that no one can catch up to him! And after a swim? He makes his way over to his best friend Surfito's house to have a snackito and tell her about all his latest swimming adventures.

○ Chillito™

○ Cloudito™

○ Flippito™

● Houndito™

○ Huskito™

○ Luvito™

MILD

MEDIUM

HOT

Super Rare

SUPER SPICY

◐ **Muddito**™

● **Pinkito**™

○ **Rapidito**™

○ **Tabbito**™

○ **Tuskito**™

○ **Wildito**™

Name: Chillito ™

Birthday: January 20

Super Rare

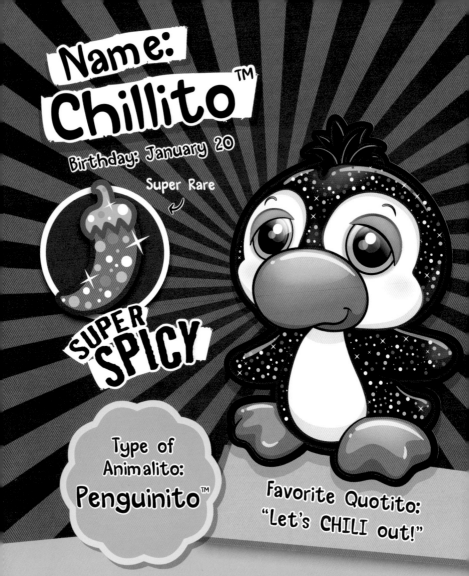

SUPER SPICY

Type of Animalito:
Penguinito ™

Favorite Quotito:
"Let's CHILI out!"

Secret Factito

Chillito loves having frienditos over to hang out. She's a really thoughtful Penguinito and has extra blanketitos for her frienditos who prefer a warmer temperature. Her favorite time of year is winter during a freezing cold snowstorm. She loves making snow angelitos and building snow castles!

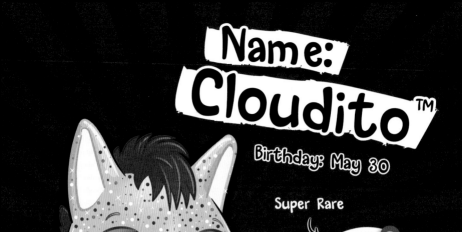

Name: Cloudito™

Birthday: May 30

Super Rare

SUPER SPICY

Favorite Quotito:
"Believe in MAGICITO!"

Type of Animalito:
Pegasito™

Secret Factito

Cloudito is one of the most magical Cutetitos in the worldito! At night when she flies through the clouds, her sparkles shine extra brightito. Sometimes Cutetitos watching from the ground below think she's a shooting star passing by and make a wish! Cloudito hopes all their wishes come true!

Name:
Flippito™

Birthday: March 22

Super Rare

SUPER
SPICY

Type of
Animalito:
Sealito™

Favorite Quotito:
"GUAC your socks off!"

Secret Factito

Flippito loves to dance, even though he might not be the best dancer. Whenever there is music playing, Flippito is dancing like no one's watching! He even invented a dance move called the Flip Flopito, which is now the latest craze! Well, so far he is the only one to do it, but he's confident it will catch on soonito!

Name:
Houndito™

Birthday: May 6

MEDIUM

Favorite Quotito:
"Sugar, SPICE, and everything nice!"

Type of Animalito:
Puppito™

Secret Factito

Houndito has a sweet tooth and loves baking goodies to share with her frienditos. Her peanut butter cookies are her specialty, but she also enjoys baking muffins, cupcakes, pies . . . really anything that's yumito!

Name:
Huskito™

Birthday: September 1

MILD

Type of
Animalito:
Puppito™

Favorite Quotito:
"I'm the TACO the town!"

Secret Factito

Hollywood can't stop talking about the newest star of the
silver screen—Huskito! He has walked the red carpetito
and signed many autographitos. He's ready to star in more
comedies and dramas for all his frienditos to see.

Name: Luvito™

Birthday: February 20

MILD

Favorite Quotito:
"I'm a HUGGITO machine!"

Type of
Animalito:
Chihuahito™

Secret Factito

Luvito's birthday is so close to Valentine's Day, it is no wonder she has so much love to give her frienditos! Her favorite shape is a heart, of course, and her favorite giftito to give (and receive) is a huggito. This Chihuahito is so loving, kind, and sweet, there really is no other Cutetito quite like her!

Name: Muddito™

Birthday: June 29

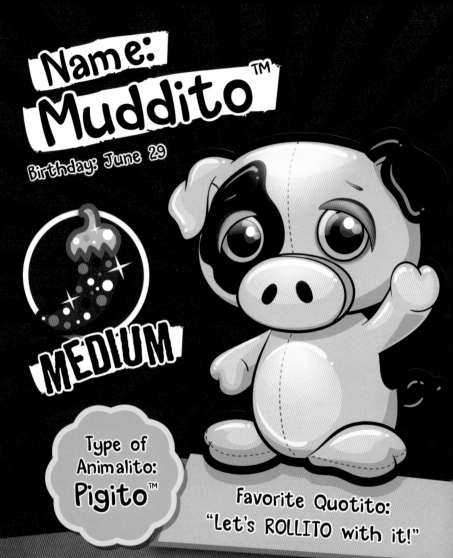

MEDIUM

Type of
Animalito:
Pigito™

Favorite Quotito:
"Let's ROLLITO with it!"

Secret Factito

Muddito's idea of a relaxing self-care day is applying his
signature mud maskito and then rolling around in some more
mud. At first his frienditos didn't want to try his spa routine,
but once they did, their skin was super softito! Now there
is a waiting list for his signature mud maskito, but Muddito
doesn't mind—he is just happy to share his love of mud!

MEDIUM

Favorite Quotito:
"I'm your biggest FANITO!"

Type of
Animalito:
Flamingito™

Secret Factito

Pinkito loves fangirling over her favorite staritos. She tries to get selfies with all her favorite actors and is always the first in line for her favorite bands' concertitos. If you ever need a friend to join you on the red carpetito or have an extra ticketito for a show, Pinkito is the one to call!

Name: Rapidito™

Birthday: December 4

HOT

Type of Animalito: **Cheetarito**™

Favorite Quotito: "Give it all you've GUAC!"

Secret Factito

Rapidito is a major sports fan who enjoys playing all sorts of games and cheering on her frienditos from the stands. Her favorite sport is cross-country running, because she is super fastito! This year, Rapidito is competing in the Cutetitos Relay Race. This Cheetarito hopes to bring home the goldito, but she will be proud of herself either way!

Name:
Tabbito™

Birthday: April 30

MILD

Favorite Quotito:
"TACO about awesome!"

Type of
Animalito:
Catito™

Secret Factito

Tabbito knows that the key to a good partito is great foodito. Breakfast, lunch, dinner, dessert, snacks, and more—Tabbito has a favorite dish for it all. He loves sharing his treats with his frienditos, but he won't share his recipes! Shh—they're family secrets!

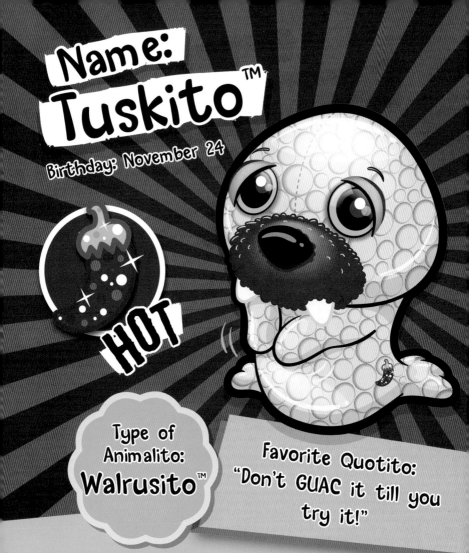

Name: Tuskito™

Birthday: November 24

HOT

Type of Animalito: Walrusito™

Favorite Quotito: "Don't GUAC it till you try it!"

Secret Factito

This Walrusito is a very crafty Cutetito. With so many hobbies, he can't choose one he likes best! He hosts a weekly book clubito, collects stampitos, and even sews his own quiltitos! Do you want to start a knitting club? Or maybe even try a pottery class? Tuskito will absolutely be your craft-time buddito!

Name: Wildito™

Birthday: January 31

HOT

Favorite Quotito:
"You're BURRITOFUL inside and out!"

Type of Animalito:
Zebrito™

Secret Factito

Wildito sees the beauty inside all his frienditos and can make them look their best when they're ready for a makeoverito. He likes styling hair and doing makeup, especially if the Cutetito he is styling loves their new look! When it comes to his own style, this Zebrito likes to change things up pretty often. One day he can dress preppy and the next like a punk rockerito!

○ Brainito™ ● Cheezito™ ● Chippito™

○ Hungrito™ ○ Kittito™ ○ Maskito™

MILD

MEDIUM

HOT

Super Rare

SUPER SPICY

Quackito™

Sleepito™

Spookito™

Spottito™

Stinkito™

Tallito™

↖ Super Rare

SUPER
SPICY

Type of
Animalito:
Owlito™

Favorite Quotito:
"Time for hugs and
BABITO snugs!"

Secret Factito

Even though she isn't old enough for school yet, Brainito is
getting a head start on her studies. She'd rather learn a new
fact about the world than play outside with the other Babitos.
There's just so much to study if she's going to be the smartest

Name:
Cheezito ™

Birthday: June 4

MEDIUM

Favorite Quotito:
"I'm the boss BABITO!"

Type of
Animalito:
Mousito™

Secret Factito

Cheezito is one bossy Babito, and he *almost* always gets
what he wants. He has the latest toys and can usually be
found eating his favorite cheese treats. Sometimes he can
get a little squeaky if he doesn't get what he wants, though!
If you're babysitting this little Babito, make sure you let him
know who's *really* in charge (and maybe have his favorite
treats on handito, just in case).

Name:
Chippito™

Birthday: September 23

MEDIUM

Type of Animalito:
Chipmunkito™

Favorite Quotito:
"New BABITO on the block!"

Secret Factito

Chippito is already exploring the world around him—he wasn't born yesterday! When his first tooth came in, he was finally able to try an acornito for the first time, and he loved it. Now he has a whole stash of acornitos hidden around the neighborhood for an on-the-go snack no matter where his

Name:
Hungrito™

Birthday: February 15

HOT

Favorite Quotito:
"BABITOS gotta eat!"

Type of Animalito:
Hippotito™

Secret Factito

Hungrito has an appetite-ito that never seems to go away!
Once he's finished his meal, he's ready for the next, especially
if it's ice cream with rainbow sprinkle-itos. He's a really messy
eater, but that just means he's enjoying his food. This hungry
Hippotito loves eating so much, his first word was "yumito"!

Name:
Kittito ™

Birthday: August 8

HOT

Type of Animalito:
Catito ™

Favorite Quotito:
"Nobody puts BABITO in the corner!"

Secret Factito

She may seem like a sweet little Babito, but don't let her looks fool you—Kittito is more than just a pretty kitty. She's ready to be treated like a full-grown Catito! Don't make baby talkito noises at her, and definitely don't try to tickle her—her scratch

Name:
Maskito™

Birthday: November 23

Super Rare

SUPER
SPICY

Favorite Quotito:
"I'll always be your BABITO!"

Type of Animalito:
Raccoonito™

Secret Factito

Maskito loves being a Babito so much, he never wants to grow up! He thinks being a Babito is the best because all he has to do is play, cuddle, take burrito naps, and eat his favorite fooditos—what else could a Raccoonito want? Of course, he has to grow up some day, but for now he's happy being taken care of.

Name:
Quackito™

Birthday: January 18

MILD

Type of
Animalito:
Duckito™

Favorite Quotito:
"Ice, ice BABITO!"

Secret Factito

Quackito's got rhythmito! Whenever she hears music playing,
she quacks to the beat and flaps her wings. She loves songs
that rhyme and knows how to quack along to any beat.

Name:
Sleepito™

Birthday: March 14

Super Rare

SUPER
SPICY

Favorite Quotito:
"GUAC-a-bye BABITO!"

Type of
Animalito:
Sheepito™

Secret Factito

Sleepito loves taking long burrito naps and can cozy up and fall asleep pretty much anywhere! One time, she fell asleep while she was at a loud rock concertito! Nothing can stop this sleepy Sheepito from chasing her dreams . . . literally!

Name:
Spookito™

Birthday: April 17

MEDIUM

Type of
Animalito:
Battito™

Favorite Quotito:
"Peek-a-boo, BABITO!"

Secret Factito

Spookito's favorite game is hide-and-seekito, but with a twist—when you find her, BOO, she scares you! Spookito doesn't scare easily, but one night she lost her burrito blanket and was very frightened that she would never see it again. Luckily, she found it and was able to fall asleep and dream her favorite nightmares that same night.

Name:
Spottito™

Birthday: October 1

MILD

Favorite Quotito:
"TACO about a cute BABITO!"

Type of Animalito:
Puppito™

Secret Factito

Spottito is the happiest Puppito around—he smiles! It's really easy to make him laughito: Just make a funny face or tickle behind his ear, and he'll let out a really cute chuckle. He is happiest when he gets a new toy, and he loves meeting new frienditos to share his toys with.

Name:
Stinkito™

Birthday: June 14

MILD

Type of
Animalito:
Skunkito™

Favorite Quotito:
"It's adventure time,
BABITO!"

Secret Factito

Stinkito may be a tiny Babito, but he pulls off some epic
stuntitos! He'll jump over toys without hesitation, and he
even knows a few karate kickitos. One day he'll be an action
starito, but for now he's just a fearless, super-cute Skunkito!

Tallito™

Birthday: May 30

HOT

Favorite Quotito:
"Hasta la vista, BABITO!"

Type of Animalito:
Giraffito™

Secret Factito

Ever since Tallito was born, she's been running around wild! This Giraffito comes from a long line of champion runners. It can be hard to catch her, but once you do, be prepared to chase her all over again—she won't sit still for long! The only time you'll see Tallito stay in one place is when she's having a snack. All that running makes her very hungrito!

Poster FUN!

Cut along the dotted lines for double-sided

posters featuring your favorite Cutetitos!

Ask an adult for help with cutting along the dotted lines!

© 2020 Basic Fun, Inc.

© 2020 Basic Fun, Inc.